emmeline's tooth

The Scritchy Little
Twitchell Sisters

With love for my sister, Elizabeth Garn;
for the Twitchell Sisters, Louisa and Emma Thanhauser;
for Rhoda and Frances, Doris and Muriel, Lynn and Jane,
Leslie and Laurie, Jan and Jill, and Nancy and Patti. — L.A.G.

For Charlie and Jennifer. *Never* scritchy! — E.B.

Text copyright 2001 by Laura Aimee Garn
Illustrations copyright 2004 by Erik Brooks
Designer: Jacqueline Kachman, Kachman Design
Editor: Nancy Parent
The text of this book is set in 12 pt. Bodoni Book
The illustrations are rendered in pen and ink with watercolor.

Pretty Please Press, Inc. 105 East 29th Street, 6th Floor New York, New York 10016
First Edition
10 9 8 7 6 5 4 3 2 1
Printed in U.S.A.

Library of Congress Control Number: 2004195156
ISBN Hardcover: 0-9759378-1-2
ISBN Paperback edition: 0-9759378-6-3

Many years ago in the village of Ganderbury, there lived a family called the Twitchells. Mr. and Mrs. Twitchell had a lovely baby girl named Lavinia. And not long after Lavinia was born, they were blessed with a second daughter, Emmeline.

"Isn't your sister adorable, Lavinia?" asked Mrs. Twitchell. "She'll be your playmate, your friend, and your companion."

"Blech, yetch, phooey," growled Lavinia, who spoke very well for two years of age. "I'm going to bite off all her toes."

Emmeline just gurgled and smiled, but Mr. Twitchell quickly moved the cradle out of Lavinia's reach.

The girls grew up to be quite different. Lavinia had black hair and blue eyes; Emmeline had blond hair and brown eyes. Lavinia was tall and strong, while Emmeline was tiny and delicate. Lavinia loved lavender, cream puffs, and her pet gecko, El. Emmeline loved sky blue, raspberries, and her pet potto, Lorenzo.

Mr. and Mrs. Twitchell were surprised to find that their daughters, who looked angelic, were really very testy. Whenever the girls played together, they fought. Most of their dolls had no arms, and their toys were in pieces.

By the time Lavinia was five years old, and Emmeline was three, the girls were at war. They would start at breakfast, squabbling over whose piece of toast was larger or who had more nuggets of Mushy Mallow cereal in her bowl.

7

They quarreled as they dressed.

"My dress is prettier," taunted Lavinia in a singsong voice.

"Not anymore," Emmeline replied, ripping her sister's sleeve.

"Emmeline is wearing my hair ribbons," snarled Lavinia.

"No, they're mine," cried Emmeline with a pinch, a slap, and a shriek.

They pummeled each other outside.

"I want the swing!" Lavinia shouted, shoving Emmeline out of the way.

Emmeline pushed her sister into a mud puddle.

"MAMA! Emmeline ruined my shoes."

"Lavinia's a snitch, an itchy little snitch."

After a morning of play, Mrs. Twitchell had to rest with a cold compress on her head and a soothing cup of tea.

Mr. and Mrs. Twitchell reasoned with the girls.

"You must take turns," they insisted. "You must share and be considerate of each other."

For a moment the girls would be quiet, as if considering their parents' wisdom. Then they would pick up right where they left off.

The Twitchells pleaded and punished, begged and bribed, threatened and cajoled.

The girls slapped and pulled, scratched and shook, bellowed and shrieked.

When the sisters fought in public, crowds gathered. Their parents were mortified. Friends and neighbors were concerned.

TODAY'S
SERMON

I AM NOT
MY BROTHER'S
KEEPER

Eventually they divided the household. Mrs. Twitchell and
Lavinia lived in one half of the house, while Mr. Twitchell and Emmeline
stayed in the other. All their clothes and toys were carefully separated,
labeled, and locked away.

Mrs. Twitchell took Lavinia to morning classes, dancing lessons, and to tea with her Aunt Isabella.

Mr. Twitchell took Emmeline to afternoon classes, piano lessons, and to visit Uncle Otto and his bulldogs.

When the girls were asleep, Mr. and Mrs. Twitchell met in
the parlor.

"Did you pay the greengrocer for the melons Lavinia threw at
Emmeline yesterday?" Mrs. Twitchell asked one night.

"Yes," Mr. Twitchell replied. "Quite expensive. The girls' fighting is
taking a toll on the family pocketbook and on my nerves. Their voices are
so… scritchy."

"Don't you mean 'screechy,' dear?" asked Mrs. Twitchell.

"Perhaps I do," said Mr. Twitchell. "But 'scritchy' suits them."

Then Mrs. Twitchell noticed an advertisement in the Ganderbury Gazette. "Look, Harold," she said. "Travelstead's Variety Show is coming to the Music Hall next Saturday. Could we go?"

"Oh, yes," said Mr. Twitchell. "Why don't you go with Lavinia, and I'll take Emmeline?"

"And we'll sit on opposite sides of the hall," said Mrs. Twitchell. "Perhaps Lavinia and I will sit in the balcony, just to be safe."

At Travelstead's Variety Show, the highlight of the program was
the extraordinary magician, Umberto the Great. He poured water into
a top hat and pulled out a rabbit. He reached into his sleeve and found a
bunch of tulips.

When he waved a white scarf over a basket of eggs, doves flew
into the air. After he made his assistant disappear, Umberto turned to the
audience.

"I now require a volunteer to assist me." He pointed to Emmeline in
the fifth row. "Come here, my dear. Don't be shy."

Emmeline walked onto the stage, and the magician seated her with a flourish. Suddenly there was a ruckus in the balcony.

"Wait, Mr. Magician!" called Lavinia, bolting out of her seat. "*I'm* your volunteer."

"You are not!" shrieked Emmeline. "He picked *me*!"

Lavinia stomped onto the stage, took the magician's water pitcher and drenched her sister.

"Don't you have to change your dress, Drippy?" she bellowed.

Emmeline snatched the basket of eggs and pelted Lavinia.

"Don't you have to change, too, Miss Grabby?"

"Now, now, ladies," said Umberto.

Mr. and Mrs. Twitchell dashed onto the stage, picked up their soggy, squealing daughters, and dragged them up the aisle.

"If he were a really good magician, he might have made them both disappear!" said Mr. Twitchell.

EMMELINE IS
EXCELLENT

LAVINIA

TWITCHELL

BRINGS DOWN
THE HOUSE!!

Mr. Travelstead met the Twitchells on their way out the door.

"We apologize," said Mr. Twitchell. "We'll pay for all the damages."

"Damages?" said Mr. Travelstead. "Listen to that audience! They're howling. To you the girls' squabbling is horrible, but to the audience it's hilarious! Your daughters could join my company on tour. Think about it — their names on the marquee. Fame, fortune, exotic travel. We'll be in Dubuque next week."

"What do we have to do?" asked Mr. Twitchell.

"Nothing… I'll dress the stage, and the girls will do what comes naturally. I'll draw up a contract right away."

"I want the fanciest costume," said Lavinia briskly. "Feathers, sequins, flounces. And my name should be first in the program."

"I'm the prettiest, so mine goes first," said Emmeline.

"Welcome to our theatrical family," said Mr. Travelstead.

When the Twitchells arrived at the theater the next day,
Mr. Travelstead was ready for them.

"Profiting from their awful behavior doesn't seem right," said
Mr. Twitchell.

"Nonsense," said Mr. Travelstead. "Now, girls… I have devised a
little scene with a birthday theme. When are yours?"

"Mine is March 28th," said Lavinia.

"It's always Lavinia's birthday," wailed Emmeline. "It's never mine."

"Just as I thought," said Mr. Travelstead. "Here is your set. Let's
see what you can do."

Onstage sat two cakes: a chocolate one with fat pink roses and a vanilla with marzipan butterflies.

"Gimme those butterflies!" screeched Lavinia.

"You smashed my marzipan!" cried Emmeline.

As a musician played "Happy Birthday to You," Lavinia and Emmeline trounced the cakes, shredded their dresses and slipped on the gooey icing. At the finale, there were fireworks.

"Brava, brava!" Mr. Travelstead cried. "I don't know how you live with them, but they are a spectacle."

"The Scritchy Little Twitchell Sisters" went on tour with
Travelstead's Variety Show. Mr. Travelstead carefully prepared the sets and
props. There were cakes, fancy dresses, a life-sized Pachisi game, a shiny
new bicycle, and a scooter. Onstage, the girls behaved as they always had,
to standing-room-only crowds.

24

"Gimme that! Out of my way!" they screamed. *Pinch, slap, ouch!*
"It's mine, bratty. You're a stinker!" *Kick, stomp, yelp.*

Their notices were excellent: "Slugging Sisters a Smashing
Success," said the Vaudeville Review. "Road to Riches Paved with
Pinches" and "Pinch Her Perfect" the Gazette headlines raved.

Life with the touring variety show was busy and exciting. The
Twitchell Sisters had to rehearse and perform, keep up their schoolwork,
and practice their dance routines.

After several months of touring, however, the girls seemed to change.

"I miss being at home," Lavinia complained one day. "How is
Emmeline doing?"

"She's fine, dear," Mrs. Twitchell replied. "Why do you ask?"

"I never see her except onstage."

"You don't miss her, do you?" said her mother.

"Not at all," sniffed Lavinia.

Emmeline also had some curious moments.

"I didn't hurt Lavinia when I pushed her off the bicycle, did I?" she asked her father.

"Of course not, Emmeline," Mr. Twitchell said. "The stage is perfectly safe. You weren't worried, were you?"

"Worried?" said Emmeline. "About *her*? Ha!"

"All is well, dear," he said. "You're squabbling beautifully."

One night the girls were onstage with a new set — Mr. Travelstead had designed a game of croquet on a lawn with a birdbath for the water fight.

"I saw you cheat!" Emmeline cried. "You nudged the ball with your foot!"

Lavinia blinked. "You're right; I did. I'm very sorry. It's your turn."

"Splash the water, Emmeline," the director hissed. "Get closer."

Instead, Emmeline played through. "Your turn," she told Lavinia.

"I've been thinking, Emmeline," said Lavinia. "I've been unfair. I wouldn't be here if it weren't for you."

"We wouldn't be here without each other," said Emmeline. "I'm lonely. I'd like to have a sister to play with."

"I would, too," Lavinia admitted.

"This is the day I've been waiting for," said Mrs. Twitchell tearfully.

"This is the day I've been dreading," said Mr. Travelstead, as Lavinia and Emmeline hugged each other.

"Curtain down!"

After that evening, the Twitchell Sisters' theatrical fortunes declined rapidly. At the next show, they gave each other pieces of birthday cake with the biggest butterflies and roses. The Gazette reported on this strange development with a new story: "Squabbling Sisters' Success Scuttled by Curious Consideration."

"They've lost the magic," said Mr. Travelstead. "You gain a peaceful household and I lose an act."

"We have enjoyed working with you," said Mr. Twitchell. "But I think we're all ready to go home."

"I never dared dream that this day would come," said Mrs. Twitchell, watching the girls play badminton one summer afternoon.

Mr. Twitchell smiled. "I think our girls finally realized that they needed each other for *more* than the act. After all, growing and changing is what children do best."

"I must say, I do miss having little ones," said Mrs. Twitchell wistfully.

"We *could* have another baby, Mathilda," said Mr. Twitchell.

"We could, indeed, Harold," said Mrs. Twitchell. "Maybe even two. But what if they turned out to be as 'scritchy' as Lavinia and Emmeline?"

"Then we'll be the 'Happy Scritchy Twitchell Family,'" said Mr. Twitchell.

And so they were.